MW00905331

*FIRST FLIGHT® is an exciting
new series of beginning readers.
The series presents titles which include songs,
poems, adventures, mysteries, and humour
by established authors and illustrators.
FIRST FLIGHT® makes the introduction to
reading fun and satisfying
for the young reader.*

*FIRST FLIGHT® is available in 4 levels
to correspond to reading development.*

Level 1 – Preschool - Grade 1
Large type, repetition of simple concepts that are
perfect for reading aloud, easy vocabulary and
endearing characters in short simple stories for
the earliest reader.

Level 2 – Grade 1 - Grade 3
Longer sentences, higher level of vocabulary, repetition, and
high-interest stories for the progressing reader.

Level 3 – Grade 2 - Grade 4
Simple stories with more involved plots and a simple chapter
format for the newly independent reader.

Level 4 – Grade 3 - up (First Flight Chapter Books)
More challenging level, minimal illustrations for the
independent reader.

For my friend, Viji

Thanks to the following people:
my family, Ian, Karen and Robin,
for their unfailing support and encouragement;
Karleen Bradford, Jan Andrews, Caroline Parry
and Alice Bartels, for their helpful suggestions;
the many Grade 5/6 kids at Trillium Elementary School,
Cumberland, Ontario, for their interest and input;
Melanie Colbert, for her encouragement,
and for finding a good home for Fangs;
and most of all, Dr. Charles Dondale, whose love and lore
of spiders was invaluable to bringing Fangs *to life.*

RG

FANGS AND ME

FIRST FLIGHT® is a registered trademark of Fitzhenry & Whiteside.

First published in the United States in 1999.

Fitzhenry & Whiteside acknowledges with thanks the support of the
Government of Canada through its Book Publishing Industry Development
Program in the publication of this title.

Printed in Canada.

Design by Wycliffe Smith Design

10 9 8 7 6 5 4 3 2 1

Canadian Cataloguing in Publication Data

Gilmore, Rachna, 1953-
Fangs & me

(A first flight chapter book)
ISBN 1-55041-512-3

I. Gordon Sauve. II. Title. III. Title: Fangs and me. IV. Series.

PS8563.I57F36 1999   jC813'.54   C99-930030-X
PZ7.G54Fa 1999

A First Flight® Chapter Book

FANGS AND ME

By Rachna Gilmore
Illustrated by Gordon Sauvé

Fitzhenry & Whiteside • Toronto

CHAPTER
[ONE]

I stood at the bottom of my driveway and waved and waved at the car taking away Veena. When it turned the corner, I just stood there like a dummy, waving to an empty street.

Mom patted my shoulder. "Never mind, Maisie," she said cheerfully. "You'll make new friends."

I forced down the lump in my throat and blinked hard. Sometimes I'm glad I wear glasses.

Mom breezed on, "Look on the bright side, Maisie, you're not moving — you know other kids from school. Just call someone. All you have to do is get over your shyness, have a bit of courage."

Dad bent down and hugged me. He's kind of chubby and he has a big soft stomach. He said, "I know you'll miss her, Maisie. She was a good friend."

I squeezed him hard. Dad understands. He never says the kind of fake cheery things Mom does to make you feel better.

Mom went on, "Anyway, the new family is moving in today, and they have a son your age. You'll be friends in no time."

Mom, she's like a steamroller. She can't understand anyone being different. She tries to help, but the trouble is, she usually doesn't.

My glasses were getting steamy, so I pulled away from Dad and cleared my throat.

Mom said briskly, "Well, I'm going inside."

62 Hummingbird Drive, Veena's house, looked lost and lonely. How could the sun shine so brightly, like it was any regular summer day?

Veena and I'd been best friends for five years. Sure, I knew other kids, but I'd never hung out with anyone else. I'm not good at going up to kids and starting conversations. Or phoning them. What would I say? They'd think I was dumb, I know they would. A lot of people do, just because I'm quiet on the outside. Veena, she understood me. She liked me, quiet and all. And she never freaked out about my spiders.

I let out a long sigh. What was going to be worse — the rest of the summer without Veena, or school?

Dad put his hand on my shoulder. I tried to smile. It came out kind of wobbly.

"Sometimes life's tough, Maisie, and you just have to get through it."

I was so glad he wasn't trying to cheer me up that I actually felt a bit better.

"Want to work on that mountain with me?" asked Dad.

Dad and I were putting together this enormous puzzle of Mount Everest. It took forever to find the right pieces — one bit of mountain looked a lot like another.

"Nah, I don't think so, Dad. I'll just kick around the yard."

I wandered around the side of the house.

The swing sat there empty. It hung from an old maple tree that was half in our yard, and half in Veena's. Dad and Veena's father, Mr. Sharma, put it up five years ago, when they moved here. I couldn't swing on it, not right now.

I went over to the dogwood bushes in the backyard to look for spiders. I started to peer through the branches, looking for webs. Somehow, I couldn't see straight. I ran towards the door, half-planning to go cry in my room.

And that's when I saw her. A spider on the middle of a huge web between the lilac bush and

the railing of the back doorstep. She was just gorgeous. I forgot all about crying and went up close.

It was an orb web and the spider was yellowy-brown with a white cross on her abdomen. With her legs outstretched, she was almost seven centimeters across, the biggest I'd ever seen. A real beauty.

Mom came out with a basket of laundry. "What're you looking at?"

I pointed. The spider sat still and stared at me. Actually, I knew she didn't — spiders don't see too well — but it *seemed* like she stared at me.

Mom chuckled. "Wow, it looks like it belongs in a haunted house."

"She," I said. "A female spider has smaller pedipalps, these leg-like things behind the mouth."

Mom peered at the spider. "Well, she sure is fierce-looking."

"Oh, she's not, she's a diadem spider, see the cross? And they're kind of scaredy-cat spiders, really. She…"

Mom held up her hand, "No, no, don't tell me."

She isn't at all interested in spiders, but at least she doesn't mind them.

The spider sat still, each leg shifting slowly from one web strand to another — waiting for a movement to tell her an insect had landed. Spread out like that, she looked big and tough. "I'll call you Fangs," I said to her. "That's a tough name for a scaredy-cat spider."

"Call who Fangs?" asked Dad, coming out the back door. He had a glass of lemonade in one hand and a newspaper in the other.

He stopped when he saw Fangs.

"Oh...right. Nice," he said, trying not to squeak. He came slowly down the stairs, on the side farthest from her web, but his eyes never left Fangs. They had this glazed look, like he was hypnotized.

Dad never *says* he doesn't like spiders, but I can tell. It's funny, a lot of people are like that. I mean, some of the kids in school think I'm a freak, just because *I* don't freak out when I see spiders. I don't get it. I've always loved spiders.

I got my spider jar from the house and put it over Fangs. Gently, I tapped her from the back of the web. She fell into the jar. I tipped her onto my hand. She scurried across my palm and over to the back of my hand. I loved the tickling movements. I put out two fingers from my other hand in front of her, like a bridge, and she scampered across. I let her move from one hand to the other for a while, then put her back in the jar with a leafy twig so she wouldn't dry out. I screwed on the lid which I'd punched with holes.

"You okay in there, Fangs?" I asked softly. "Don't worry, I'll put you back on your web soon, I just want to look at you."

Fangs sat still.

"See, you've made a new friend already," said Mom chirpily.

I sighed.

"If you can make friends with a spider, I'm sure you can with kids."

Mom just didn't understand. It was easy talking to spiders. It was a lot harder talking to kids.

It was going to be an awfully quiet and dull three weeks before school started, I thought.

But I couldn't have been more wrong.

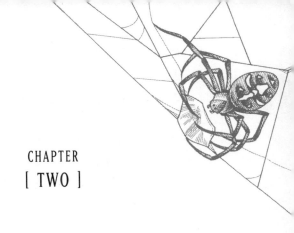

CHAPTER
[TWO]

It was late in the afternoon. I'd put Fangs
back on her web and she was hiding from
the heat, in her nest — some leaves at the
edge of the web she'd tied together with
silk. I was so busy watching her that I forgot about Veena, about everything, until I
heard a truck.

I peered around the side of the house.

A car pulled into the driveway next door
and a huge moving van stopped out front.

I watched the movers set up a ramp to
the back of the van and start to unload the
furniture.

The heaviness in my chest grew tighter. I
didn't know what I hated more — Veena's
house being empty, or strangers in it.

I ran inside, up to my room, and shut the door.

I slumped down at my desk in front of the window. Funny, I'd never minded being alone before. I'd never felt lonely.

Make new friends, Mom said. Easy for her.

Kelly. I knew her. She didn't really belong with any group, but everyone liked her. A few times Veena had invited her over and the three of us had played together. But it was always Veena who'd called her. I shut my eyes and imagined me in the schoolyard. I screwed up my courage. Heart thumping, I walked towards Kelly. She turned to look at me. Then she burst out laughing and ran away. "Beat it," she shouted.

I opened my eyes. My mouth was dry. If I couldn't even *imagine* going up to Kelly, how was I going to *talk* to other kids?

From the corner of my eye, I saw someone in Veena's backyard.

I leaned forward to get a better look.

A boy. The new kid next-door. He was supposed to be nine, just my age, but he looked awfully big. He wore baggy shorts, and a scruffy looking T-shirt. His back was to me, so I couldn't see his face, but his hair was long and blond.

The boy picked up stones and started to hit the spruce tree. Great. A stone-throwing boy. He was aiming at one of the thicker branches.

Thwack, the stone hit the tree. A flurry of black raced along the branch.

I stood up, heart pounding.

A squirrel?

Had the boy seen it? Is that what he'd been aiming at? A cold shiver crawled up my back.

CHAPTER
[THREE]

The next afternoon Mom said, "Let's go over and say hello to our new neighbors."

"Good idea," said Dad.

I didn't want to say hello to anyone, especially not the strangers in Veena's house. And definitely not a boy who'd thrown stones at a squirrel.

"I think I'll go look for Fangs," I said.

"Maisie," said Mom, "I really want you to come. We must do everything we can to make our new neighbors welcome." It was her most steamrollery voice.

Dad whispered to me, "You have to meet them some time, Maisie. Come on. Get it over with, it'll be easier."

Mom got a plateful of pumpkin-raisin

cookies Dad had baked, and we went over to Veena's front door.

I felt a sharp pang. This really wasn't Veena's house anymore — I always used to run through the shrubby part between our yards, to the back door.

A tall, thin woman opened the door. She was sort of faded, and she looked worried and tired.

"Hi, we're the Dexters, from next door." Mom held out the plate. "We just came by to say hello and see if there's anything we can do to help."

The woman smiled and her whole face softened.

"Thank you," she said. "I'm Laura Hickens. Please come in. No, you must."

There were packing boxes everywhere, things half out, piles of kitchen stuff on the table.

Mr. Hickens was moving things around. He was burly and balding, and he had a gruff voice. He shook hands with Mom and Dad and me.

"Buddy," called Mrs. Hickens. "Come on down."

Buddy. The boy's name.

You'll be friends in no time, Mom had said. I sat very still.

Buddy came thundering down the stairs.

He was big all right. Even for his age. I'm short, the shortest one in my class, so he was way bigger than I was.

I sneaked a look at him while Mrs. Hickens introduced us.

He had blue eyes and long blond hair that he kept flicking off his forehead with a toss of his head.

"Hello, Buddy," said Mom. "Nice to meet you."

Buddy shuffled his feet until Mr. Hickens nudged him. Then he looked up, smiled politely and muttered hello.

"Looks like you and Maisie are going to be in the same grade, Buddy," said Mr. Hickens.

Flick. Another smile. "That's great."

Then they were all talking about where to shop and stuff like that. I took another look at Buddy. Kids threw stones all the time — had he seen that squirrel? He had an innocent face.

But there was something about it that

made me squirm. What was it?

It was that smile. It was too...pasted on. It didn't reach his eyes.

"Buddy is a big sports fan," said Mrs. Hickens. "Especially basketball. Do you do any sports, Maisie?"

I shook my head. I knew I should say something, but as usual, my throat was all seized up.

"She tried karate once," said Mom. "But she only got one belt before she quit. Isn't that right, Maisie?"

I nodded. I hate the way parents talk for you, but I was glad I didn't have to say anything.

"Maisie has a lot of interests, but I think her main one is spiders."

This was really embarrassing.

"Spiders?" said Mrs. Hickens. "How fascinating."

Mr. Hickens laughed. "Buddy's not too keen on spiders, are you, Bud?"

Buddy shrugged, flicked his hair back.

Mr. Hickens continued, "Anytime he finds a spider in the house, he hollers for me or his mom to get it. Isn't that right, Bud?"

Buddy flushed bright red.

I felt so sorry for him. I mean, it was awful the way Mr. Hickens said it, like it was funny. I forgot my shyness and smiled at Buddy sympathetically.

He caught my eye and scowled slightly.

His father said, "Hey now, Bud, just kidding, fella."

There was an awkward silence, then Mom said, "Maisie, why don't you take Buddy out and show him the swing?"

I knew Mom was just trying to help, but her timing kind of stank.

Mrs. Hickens nodded at me with a pleased expression. "Good idea."

I groaned silently and went to the door. Buddy came behind me, equally quiet.

"I'm sure they'll be good friends," said Mom brightly.

Yeah, right.

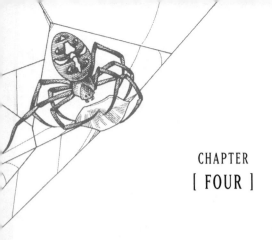

CHAPTER
[FOUR]

I led the way to the side of the house, and the trees between our yards.

"Here's the swing," I said flatly.

Buddy brushed past me, leapt onto it and started to pump up and down. He looked straight at me, his blue eyes hard.

"D'you like hockey?" he asked.

"No."

"Baseball?"

"Not really. I watch it sometimes."

Buddy rolled his eyes. I dodged aside as he swung too close to me. He was pumping higher and higher, way higher than I'd ever done.

Then, in mid-air, he jumped off, and landed a few feet in front of me.

"Betcha can't do that," he said, flicking his hair.

I moved back a little, managed to say, "I don't want to."

Buddy laughed scoffingly. "Too chicken, huh?"

I licked my lips nervously. "Just don't want to."

Buddy laughed again. "You don't play hockey, you don't play baseball, you don't even know how to swing. And *you're* the only kid on the block. Sure, we're going to be friends," he said sarcastically. "Some move this is, some wonderful move." He kicked a stone angrily. It flew towards me.

"Hey, watch it!" I cried, jumping out of the way.

"Watch it," Buddy mimicked in a high-pitched voice. "Watch it." He kicked another stone straight at me.

"Stop it, Buddy," I said.

Buddy came close to me. "Gonna make me? Shrimpy little four-eyes. *You're* gonna make me?"

My heart started to hammer.

"What're you looking at, Four-eyes?"

Buddy made a horrible face. I felt myself turning red. I couldn't help it. Buddy crossed his eyes and stuck out his tongue, making the worst face I'd ever seen — he even touched the tip of his nose with his tongue. It was totally gross.

"Cut it out, Buddy," I said.

Buddy uncrossed his eyes and shook his head disgustedly. "Aww, you're not even worth bothering with." He kicked another stone.

Just then I heard Mrs. Hickens calling. "Buddy, Maisie, come and get some lemonade."

I turned and ran inside. Buddy came thundering up beside me.

As Mrs. Hickens handed us the lemonade she said, "I'm so glad there's someone Buddy's age here."

Mr. Hickens said to Mom and Dad, "Buddy wasn't too keen on the move. You know how kids are. Had a lot of friends, back there, in Calgary, into all kinds of sports." He thumped Buddy's back. "But look, Bud, you made a new friend already, didn't you?"

Buddy made his face smile and said in a tight, polite voice, "Yeah. Thanks for showing me the swing, Maisie."

Mrs. Hickens beamed at Mom and Dad.

Buddy's blue eyes were wide and innocent.

I shivered as I forced down the sour lemonade.

CHAPTER
[FIVE]

"Well, that was lovely," said Mom brightly, as we went home. "Buddy seems like a nice boy, doesn't he, Maisie?"

Nice? I opened my mouth to tell her.

Dad looked at me anxiously and said, "It takes time to make friends, Maisie, but you made a start today. Good for you."

I closed my mouth. Dad worried about me, even though he never said it. If I told about Buddy, he'd just worry more. As for Mom, she'd probably say, *I'm sure it was a misunderstanding. Give him a chance.*

Grown-ups never understood about kids like Buddy.

I went to the back doorstep and found Fangs. She was resting in her nest at the side of the web.

In a whisper, I told her all about Buddy. "He's a real creepazoid," I said.

Fangs sat still and listened, her legs twitching gently.

Then a fly landed in Fangs' web and she rushed out. She caught the fly and bit it, killing it. She'd be busy for the next hour, squirting it with juices to help her digest the fly, then she'd suck it in.

A lot of people think it's gross, but hey, a spider's got to do what a spider's got to do.

Mom came out. "Still watching that spider?" She tilted her head to one side. "Maisie, why don't you ask Buddy over? I'm sure he'd like that. After all, he's new here; he must feel pretty lost and strange."

My chest went tight. "There's...er...there's some stuff I need to look up in my spider book," I said quickly.

I ran inside. I took out *Spiders and Their Kin*. I knew the part about diadem spiders nearly by heart, but I read it over anyway. Twice. I shut my book, then opened it again. If I went outside, Mom would try and get me to hang out with Buddy. I'd rather stay in my room all day.

The next morning, Mom went to work early. I love Mom and everything, but it was a relief having her gone. Dad, he'd never push me to call on Buddy. He sat at the kitchen table, reading the newspaper. He's a teacher, so he has the summers off.

After breakfast, I went outside to check on Fangs. It was a still, quiet morning. No one was up next door.

Fangs was on her web, finishing off an insect she'd caught. I didn't want to interrupt her, so I watched for a while, then wandered around to the side of the house, to the swing. I climbed on and started to pump slowly. Higher and higher. Where was Veena now? She never had trouble making friends. She was probably having a great time.

Suddenly, the swing yanked backward.

Thunk! I landed hard on my stomach. The air exploded out of me and my glasses flew off.

Someone had grabbed the swing from behind.

Someone — Buddy. He was laughing scornfully.

"Ha, ha, whatta wuss! You can't swing, you can't even jump, you can't do anything."

I sat up and groped around for my glasses.
Everything was blurry. I saw Buddy's
shadow reach down and pick up something.

"Looking for these, Four-eyes?"

Oh, no, he had my glasses.

"Give me back my glasses."

"Come and get 'em, Shrimp."

I squinted my eyes and stumbled after
him, "Give them back, Buddy. I mean it."

"*I mean it, I mean it,*" Buddy mimicked.
"Here Shrimpy."

I could just make out his hand holding
something. I reached for it and grabbed.

He yanked his hand away, burst out laughing. "Come on, Four-eyes, whassa matter?"

I kept grabbing and grabbing but he was
always one step ahead.

Suddenly, he stopped. He said loudly,
"Here you are, Maisie, you dropped your
glasses. Careful not to lose them again."

I put on my glasses with shaking hands.

Then I saw why Buddy had transformed
into Mr. Nice-Guy.

Mr. Hickens was standing by his back
door, scratching his head. He smiled at us
and waved.

Buddy switched on that creepy polite smile and flicked his hair. He said softly, so only I could hear, "I'd better not catch you near that swing again, Shrimp. It's mine now."

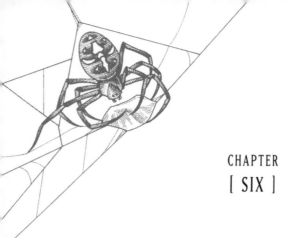

CHAPTER
[SIX]

I found Fangs, put her in the jar, and took
her up to my room. My hands were jittery for
a long while. So was my head.

What was I going to do? There were mean
kids in school, and I knew how to stay away
from them. But Buddy lived right next door.

The night before, at supper, Mom had
gone on and on about how polite he was,
how you didn't often meet kids that polite.
Telling her or Dad wasn't going to work. Not
with Buddy.

Outside, the sun blazed. I wanted to go
out, but Buddy was in his backyard, slapping
a ball around. I felt like a prisoner in my own
house.

I let Fangs out of the jar onto my hand.
She ran around over and over from one hand
to the other. It was a lovely tickling feeling. I
kept my hands loose so she wouldn't feel
cornered, even though I knew she wouldn't

bite. She looked fierce, but she was too much of a scaredy-cat. Like me. Yeah, a scaredy-cat just like me.

Well, I could hide indoors for the next few weeks, but once school started...

My heart sank. No Veena.

Just Buddy. And Mom would expect me to show him the way to school, I knew she would.

I groaned. "It's not fair, Fangs. It's so not fair. What am I going to do?"

Dad passed by my door.

"Who're you talking to, Maisie?"

Then he saw Fangs. She'd dropped on a thread from my hand and when I moved it up slowly, she came back up, like a yo-yo.

"Oh...got her in here, have you?" He swallowed and grinned nervously. "Be sure not to drop her around the house, huh? She lives outdoors." He started to move away, then turned back. "Hey, what're you doing inside on a nice day like this? Go on out. Scoot."

I sighed. Dad wanted Fangs out because he didn't like spiders, but he was right any-way. Fangs shouldn't be stuck indoors just because I was. Anyway, from the size of her, she was probably carrying eggs. She'd need to eat again soon.

I put Fangs gently back in the jar and covered the top with my hand.

Then I took a deep breath and looked out the window again.

No sign of Buddy. He must have gone in.

I was about to turn to the door, when I saw him. I stood very still.

Buddy. Buddy was sitting under the spruce tree, knees hunched up.

Suddenly, he lifted his hand and rubbed his eyes angrily.

I think my mouth dropped open.

Then Mr. Hickens came outside and shouted something.

Buddy leapt to his feet and grabbed the ball. *Thump-pump*, *thump-pump*, he whacked the ball against the tree. His whole body looked mad clear through.

I went slowly downstairs, with my hand over the top of the jar. Fangs' legs tickled the palm of my hand. I hardly noticed.

My head was all mixed up. Buddy. Hunched under that tree...had he really been crying?

CHAPTER
[SEVEN]

I put Fangs gently back on the lilac bush.
She scuttled into her leafy nest at the edge
of her web to wait for her food.

Slowly, I sat down on the back doorstep. I
stared at the bushes between my yard and
Buddy's. I could clearly see Buddy punching
the ball against the tree. *Thump-pump.*
Thump-pump. It was an angry sound. Like he
hated the whole world.

He couldn't have been crying. Not someone like Buddy. It didn't make sense. He
must have just been brushing something
from his face.

I mean, yesterday. His angry face. My
stomach went tight. And this morning —
yanking the swing out from under me, that
ugly laugh. He hadn't been crying, no way.

*Better not catch you near that swing again,
Shrimp. It's mine now.*

Suddenly, I was mad. Mad clear through.
It was not fair. That swing was mine first,
mine and Veena's. Buddy had no right, he
had no right at all.

I took in a deep breath. Buddy was not
going to stop me from swinging on it. Anyway,
Dad was right here, out in the backyard.
What could Buddy do?

I started towards the swing.

"I'll be in the kitchen, Maisie," said Dad,
going inside.

The kitchen window faced out back.

There were no windows at the side of the
house facing the swing.

My hands closed into fists. *I'm not a cow-
ard, I'm not.*

But my feet turned all by themselves, back
to the doorstep. I sat down, my knees strange-
ly wobbly. Hey, I'd rather watch Fangs than
swing. Yeah, who wanted to swing?

I felt small and hot and messy.

Fangs was too busy to bother with me.
She'd caught another insect. I couldn't make

out what it was, but it was big, and she was spinning around and around it. I felt sorry for the insect, but Fangs had to eat, too.

She did it because she had to.

Animals did that. Even a scaredy-cat spider.

For a long time I sat very still.

Me. I had to do something, too. Something about Buddy. I had to, or my life was going to be miserable.

But what? I slumped against the railing. If only I hadn't quit karate. Or if Veena was here. She would've stood up to Buddy, some-how. She was the brave one. Fangs was the only friend I had now. What could she do?

I mean, she looked fierce, but she wasn't really, not inside.

Suddenly, a picture of Buddy hunched under the tree sprang into my mind. Buddy? No, that was nuts. Buddy was as mean inside as he was outside. He was mean through and through.

I just had to find a way to stop him.

"Oh Fangs," I sighed. "If only..."

I bit my lip.

I was on my own.

CHAPTER
[EIGHT]

I woke up early the next morning. It was a gorgeous day, bright, sunny. It looked like it was going to be a scorcher later. I dressed and went downstairs. Mom had gone to work, and Dad was still in bed.

I started towards the back door, then stopped. My stomach began to twist. Buddy. I didn't have a single plan to stop him.

I caught a glimpse of myself in the mirror. I looked awfully small. I pulled myself taller. It was *my* backyard, I could go out if I wanted to. Anyway, if I stayed near the kitchen window, Buddy would leave me alone.

Wouldn't he?

My hand shook a little but I opened the door and went outside. Buddy probably wasn't even up yet.

It was all hushed and quiet with that soft, morning stillness. Peaceful. I took in a few deep breaths. I found Fangs on her web — she was usually out in the early morning and late evening, when it wasn't too hot. I dropped her into my jar then tipped her onto my hand. She moved slowly around my palm, then to my other hand when I made the bridge.

I went over to the doorstep and put Fangs on the top. When she got near the edge I gently blocked her way. Spiders move differently in the morning, more slowly, because they're cold. She was warming up with the sun. Was she bigger than before? Did that mean she was going to lay eggs soon?

I was so busy watching her that I forgot about Buddy, forgot about all my troubles.

A shadow fell across me.

"Whatchya gawking at, Four-eyes?"

I swung around.

Buddy. Carrying his basketball.

I looked at the kitchen window. Dad still wasn't up.

"Leave me alone, Buddy." My voice shook slightly.

"Leave me alone, Buddy," he mimicked. "You gonna make me?" He came closer. "What've you got there?"

When he saw Fangs, a look of disgust crossed his face. "Eew! Gross."

He lifted his basketball and aimed at Fangs.

I didn't have time to think. I jumped forward and thumped the ball away, just as it came hurtling towards Fangs.

"Hey, what did you do that for?" cried Buddy.

Fangs moved a few steps, then sat still — any other time she'd run, but with the morning coolness she was stiff and slow.

Buddy turned around to pick up the ball.

"No!" I cried. Quickly, I bent down, made a bridge with two fingers in front of Fangs. She moved onto my fingers and I cupped her loosely in my hands. I'd have to get her inside, keep her safe, I'd...

Buddy straightened up, the ball in his hand. His face was twisted into a mean smile.

My heart beat so fast I thought it would burst.

Suddenly, I was screaming. "Don't ever try that again, Buddy. Just get out of my yard."

Buddy's eyes darted to the kitchen window. "Hey, keep it down," he growled.

Of course. He didn't want anyone to hear.

I yelled, "No, I won't keep it down. And I'm not putting up with your bullying anymore. Don't you *dare* touch Fangs again, if you dare..."

Buddy was staring, staring at my hands, his face pale.

Fangs had squirmed between my fingers and dropped from a thread. I moved my hand up and she scrambled upwards again.

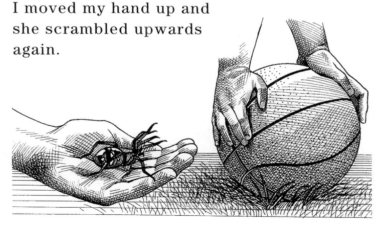

"Fangs?" Buddy had this half-amazed, half-terrified look on his face. "You really like spiders? How can you just...ugh!" It was like he couldn't take his eyes off Fangs.

I stepped forward, with Fangs on the palm of my hand.

He moved back quickly.

"Hey, keep away from me, Shrimp," he said breathlessly.

I made a bridge and moved Fangs onto my other hand. "Yeah, Buddy?" I said, casually, even though my heart was hammering. "Or what?" I took another step forward.

Buddy flushed, and moved back. "I'll...I'll...you'd better keep away, Shrimp."

"Maisie," I said, loudly. "My name's Maisie."

Buddy swallowed and licked his lips. "Yeah, whatever." His eyes flicked up. Cornered, angry. Like a fly in a web.

Suddenly I felt a bit sick. Fangs, she had no choice when she caught insects, it was instinct. But I did. I had a choice. I didn't want to become like Buddy. Not even to get back at him.

I moved away slowly. "Relax, Buddy, it's no big deal. She's not going to hurt you."

Buddy's face turned red. "Hey, I'm not afraid of spiders, I'm…"

"It's okay, my dad doesn't like spiders either; some of the kids in my class…"

Buddy sputtered, "I'm not afraid of anything, not of you, or your dumb spider, I'm not chicken, and if you…" As he spoke he quickly backed away. Then he squirmed through the bushes and disappeared into his own yard.

I put Fangs back on her web and sat down on the doorstep. My hands and knees were still trembling slightly. Bit by bit, my heartbeat slowed to normal.

Wow. I did it. I did it.

I stood up to Buddy, all by myself. Okay, with a little help from Fangs.

I grinned at her. She was sitting on her web, patiently waiting for breakfast.

Dad, wearing his tatty green dressing gown, came to the door.

"What was all that shouting about, Maisie?" he asked sleepily.

"Buddy," I said.

"What?"

I told him. I told him everything.

He let out his breath slowly. "Why on earth didn't you tell me before?"

"I didn't know if anyone would believe it. He acts so...so goody-goody with grown-ups around. Anyway, I wanted to deal with him on my own."

Dad nodded. "Sometimes, that's all it takes. Standing up to a bully." He caught me up in a fierce hug. "You're quite the kid, Maisie. You really are."

"Yeah," I grinned. "I know."

CHAPTER
[NINE]

I didn't see anything of Buddy all that day. I could hear him, at times, in his yard, but he never came near me. I played around my yard, talked to Fangs. At first I kind of kept watch over my shoulder, but after a while I was almost easy again. Almost.

The next morning I woke up early and leapt out of bed. Another beautiful, sunny day. I dressed quickly, ate my breakfast and ran outside.

Fangs was on her web, slowly moving her legs back and forth. Her abdomen was huge. She was probably going to lay her eggs soon.

I started towards the swing, then stopped. Dad wasn't up yet.

I took a deep breath and went to the swing anyway. Hey, Buddy'd left me alone yesterday, hadn't he? But I made sure I faced Buddy's house as I got on the swing.

At first my hands were kind of sweaty, and I gripped the rope too hard. Up and down, up and down, higher, higher. Slowly, my fingers relaxed. The sun was warm on my face and there was just enough of a cool breeze to lift my hair. I closed my eyes for a minute and smiled.

When I opened my eyes, my heart almost jumped out of my throat.

Buddy. Right in front of me.

I let the swing slow down. Buddy just watched me.

Finally the swing stopped.

I sat very still, my heart thumping.

Buddy kicked a stone lightly, then flicked back his hair. "Hi," he muttered.

"Hi," I managed.

He came towards me and I jumped off the swing. I started towards my backyard, then stopped. I made my knees stiff.

Buddy scowled and cleared his throat. "Look...I...yesterday, I wasn't scared or anything…" He was so big, standing there, so big. But suddenly, his face looked awfully small. "Don't go telling anyone, okay? Don't you dare go telling kids in school. I don't need anyone thinking I'm chicken or anything…"

For a moment I stared at him. Buddy. Was it possible? Was Buddy afraid about making new friends, too?

Quietly, I said, "It's okay, Buddy, I won't tell anyone. It's no big deal."

Buddy flushed bright red and blinked hard.

Suddenly, I knew. I just knew. Under that tree. Buddy had been crying, he had. Maybe it was as hard for him to move here as it was for me to lose Veena. Maybe he was a bit of a scaredy-cat as well. Like Fangs. Like me.

To my amazement, I heard myself say, "If you like, Buddy…I…I can show you the way to school, and…and tell you kids' names and stuff."

Buddy scuffed his toes in the grass and turned even redder. "Sure," he muttered. "Thanks, Maisie." He turned to leave, then

stopped abruptly. "Say, where did you learn that trick anyway?"

"What trick?"

"The...the spider. Up and down, like a yo-yo?" He looked sort of creeped-out, but also impressed.

"Oh, that. No trick. See, Fangs, it's natural for her to drop and climb on her thread. I'll..." my heart beat faster, "I'll show you sometime, if you like."

"Well. Maybe." Buddy's mouth twisted into a crooked grin. "It's a cool trick."

It was the first real smile I'd seen on his face.

Then he was gone.

I stood there until my hands stopped shaking.

Slowly, I went around the corner, back to Fangs. I told her all about it. "Isn't it weird, Fangs? In a way, it's like when people get to know you. They see you're not so tough on the inside." I squinted. "Hey, d'you think maybe Buddy and I might even be friends one day?"

I knew Fangs couldn't really hear, but it seemed like she definitely shook her head.

I started to laugh. "Yeah, well, probably not anytime soon. But at least I'm not that afraid of him anymore."

CHAPTER
[TEN]

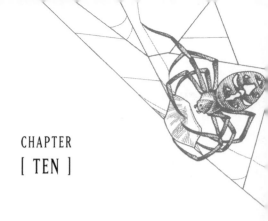

I went inside the house and got a drink of water. I grinned at myself in the mirror. Was I taller? Yes, I really thought I was.

Dad came downstairs, rubbing his eyes. "Good morning, Maisie," he said.

"Guess what, Dad? I offered to walk to school with Buddy."

Dad's eyes popped wide open. "What?"

I told him everything.

"You sure about this, Maisie?"

"Yeah, I'm sure. Hey, I can take care of myself."

Dad grinned. "I know you can. You'll make lots of new friends, too."

I'd almost forgotten about that. School. No Veena. My smile faded.

Dad's eyebrows twitched together and his forehead creased.

I drew in a long, ragged breath.

Buddy didn't know anyone here. But I did. I imagined it again. Kelly, in the schoolyard; me, nearby. My heart started to thud. I made myself go over. I said, "Hi, Kelly, want to play?" She turned around and looked at me. For the longest time. Then she smiled. "Sure, Maisie."

I felt limp all over. I could do it, I could do it. Maybe I could even call her. I'd stood up to Buddy, hadn't I, offered to walk to school with him? It *had* to be easier to call Kelly — she'd never been mean to me.

Dad was still watching me, that worried look on his face.

"It's okay, Dad. I'll make new friends."

Dad let his breath out slowly. He'd been holding it, too, just like I had.

While I was still feeling brave, I ran upstairs and grabbed my list of class numbers. I picked up the phone and dialed Kelly's number.

It was ringing. My hand was all sweaty. "Hello."

It was Kelly. I recognized her deep voice.

"Oh, hi, Kelly, it's Maisie. I was wondering, if maybe...if you're not busy...well," I forced out the words, "would you like to come over and play?"

There was a short silence. Then, "Yeah, great!" She sounded pleased. "Hey, I'm glad you called, Maisie. I was so bored. I'll tell Mom and bike right over. See ya soon."

I put the phone down with shaking hands.

I went downstairs, told Dad casually, "Kelly's coming over, okay?"

Dad's eyebrows flew up. "Sure," he said, like I had friends over everyday. I loved the way his eyes crinkled when he smiled.

I went outside and sat down in front of Fangs' web. "Wish me luck, Fangs. I invited Kelly over. I sort of know her from before, but I've never played with her without Veena."

Fangs was still waiting for her breakfast, her legs shifting on her web. I watched her as I waited for Kelly.

"Hi, Maisie."

I spun around, startled. I hadn't expected Kelly so fast.

Kelly blew her brown hair off her forehead and puffed. "I biked like crazy all the way. Hey, what are you looking at?"

I froze as Kelly came closer. Fangs. Would Kelly think I was a freak? What if she…?

Kelly's eyes widened, then lit up. "Cool. What kind is it?"

Fangs sat on her web, her legs twitching back and forth, back and forth, almost like she was waving hello.

I grinned. "Kelly, this is my friend, Fangs."

Other Books in the
First Flight® series